I saw a
BEE

A book to share from
Scallywag Press

For Stan – the boy who saw the bee

First published in Great Britain in 2019
by Scallywag Press Ltd, 10 Sutherland Row, London SW1V 4JT

Printed on FSC paper in Romania by G.Canale & C.

001

British Library Cataloguing in Publication Data available
ISBN 978-1-912650-03-3

I saw a BEE

ROB RAMSDEN

Scallywag Press Ltd

LONDON

This is me.

I looked in a box.
I saw a bee!

Buuzzzzzzzzz!

The bee saw me!

I was scared.
I chased the bee...

The bee
chased me!

Buzzzzz!

I climbed
into the box
and I hid
from the bee.

And then,
guess what?

It hid from me.

I looked for the bee,

this way . . .

. . . and that.

No bee!

No bee.

No bee . . .

I missed the bee.
Did the bee miss me?

I listened.
I heard . . .

Buzz Buzz

I followed
the sound . . .

Buzz Buzzz Buzzzzzz

Buuzzzzzzz   Buuzzzzzzzzzzzzzzzzzz

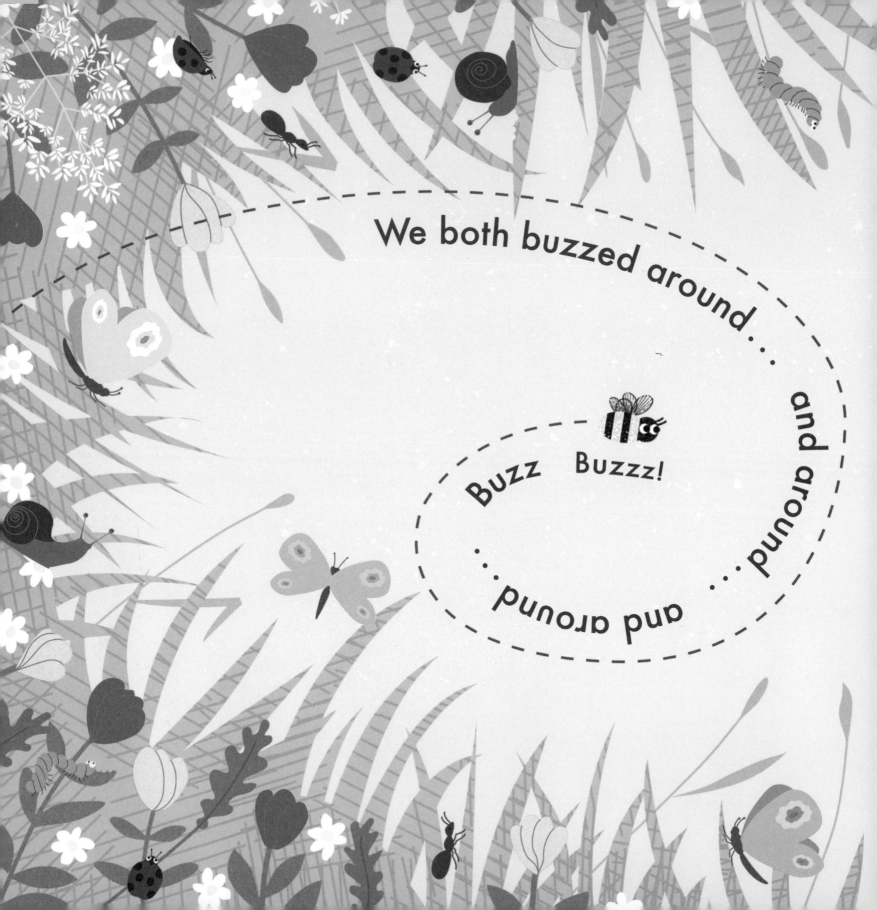

We both buzzed around… and around and around… and around

Buzz   Buzzz!

I had found the bee!

The bee had found me...

I love the bee.
The bee loves me.